Morella

By

Edgar Allan Poe

CW00841454

Itself, by itself, solely, one everlasting, and single.

PLATO: SYMPOS.

WITH a feeling of deep yet most singular affection I regarded my friend Morella. Thrown by accident into her society many years ago, my soul from our first meeting, burned with fires it had never before known; but the fires were not of Eros, and bitter and tormenting to my spirit was the gradual conviction that I could in no manner define their unusual meaning or regulate their vague intensity.

Yet we met; and fate bound us together at the altar, and I never spoke of passion nor thought of love. She, however, shunned society, and, attaching herself to me alone rendered me happy. It is a happiness to wonder; it is a happiness to dream.

Morella's erudition was profound. As I hope to live, her talents were of no common order—her powers of mind were gigantic. I felt this, and, in many matters, became her pupil. I soon, however, found that, perhaps on account of her Presburg education, she placed before me a number of those mystical writings which are usually considered the mere dross of the early German literature. These, for what reason I could not imagine, were her favourite and constant study—and that in process of time they became my own, should be attributed to the simple but effectual influence of habit and example.

In all this, if I err not, my reason had little to do. My convictions, or I forget myself, were in no manner acted upon by the ideal, nor was any tincture of the mysticism which I read to be discovered, unless I am greatly mistaken, either in my deeds or in my thoughts. Persuaded of this, I abandoned myself implicitly to the guidance of my wife, and entered with an unflinching heart into the intricacies of her studies. And then—then, when poring over forbidden pages, I felt a forbidden spirit enkindling within me—would Morella place her cold hand upon my own, and rake up from the ashes of a dead philosophy some low, singular words, whose strange meaning burned themselves in upon my memory. And then, hour after hour, would I linger by her side, and dwell upon the music of her voice, until at length its melody was tainted with terror, and there fell a shadow upon my soul, and I grew pale, and shuddered inwardly at those too unearthly tones. And thus, joy suddenly faded into horror, and the most beautiful became the most hideous, as Hinnon became Ge-Henna.

It is unnecessary to state the exact character of those disquisitions which, growing out of the volumes I have mentioned, formed, for so long a time, almost the sole conversation of Morella and myself. By the learned in what might be termed theological morality they will be readily conceived, and by the unlearned they would, at all events, be little understood. The wild Pantheism of Fichte; the modified Paliggenedia of the Pythagoreans; and, above all, the doctrines of Identity as urged by Schelling, were generally the points of discussion presenting the most of beauty to the imaginative Morella. That identity which is termed personal, Mr. Locke, I think, truly defines to consist in the saneness of rational being. And since by person we understand an intelligent essence having reason, and since there is a consciousness which always accompanies thinking, it is this which makes us all to be that which we call ourselves, thereby distinguishing us from other beings that think, and giving us our personal identity. But the principium individuations, the notion of that identity which at death is or is not lost forever, was to me, at all times, a consideration of intense interest; not more from the perplexing and exciting nature of its consequences, than from the marked and agitated manner in which Morella mentioned them.

But, indeed, the time had now arrived when the mystery of my wife's manner oppressed me as a spell. I could no longer bear the touch of her wan fingers, nor the low tone of her musical language, nor the luster of her melancholy eyes. And she knew all this, but did not upbraid; she seemed conscious of my weakness or my folly, and, smiling, called it fate. She seemed also conscious of a cause, to me unknown, for the gradual alienation of my regard; but she gave me no hint or token of its nature. Yet was she woman, and pined away daily. In time the crimson spot settled steadily upon the cheek, and the blue veins upon the pale forehead became prominent; and one instant my nature melted into pity, but in, next I met the glance of her meaning eyes, and then my soul sickened and became giddy with the giddiness of one who gazes downward into some dreary and unfathomable abyss.

Shall I then say that I longed with an earnest and consuming desire for the moment of Morella's decease?

I did; but the fragile spirit clung to its tenement of clay for many days, for many weeks and irksome months, until my tortured nerves obtained the mastery over my mind, and I grew furious through delay, and, with the heart of a fiend, cursed the days and the hours and the bitter moments, which seemed to lengthen and lengthen as her gentle life declined, like shadows in the dying of the day.

But one autumnal evening, when the winds lay still in heaven, Morella called me to her bedside. There was a dim mist over all the earth, and a warm glow upon the waters, and amid the rich October leaves of the forest, a rainbow from the firmament had surely fallen.

"It is a day of days," she said, as I approached; "a day of all days either to live or die. It is a fair day for the sons of earth and life—ah, more fair for the daughters of heaven and death!"

I kissed her forehead, and she continued:

"I am dying, yet shall I live."

"Morella!"

"The days have never been when thou couldst love me— but her whom in life thou didst abhor, in death thou shalt adore."

"Morella!"

"I repeat I am dying. But within me is a pledge of that affection—ah, how little!— which thou didst feel for me, Morella. And when my spirit departs shall the child live— thy child and mine, Morella's. But thy days shall be days of sorrow—that sorrow which is the most lasting of impressions, as the cypress is the most enduring of trees. For the hours of thy happiness are over and joy is not gathered twice in a life, as the roses of Paestum twice in a year. Thou shalt no longer, then, play the Teian with time, but, being ignorant of the myrtle and the vine, thou shalt bear about with thee thy shroud on the earth, as do the Moslemin at Mecca."

"Morella!" I cried, "Morella! How knowest thou this?" but she turned away her face upon the pillow and a slight tremor coming over her limbs, she thus died, and I heard her voice no more.

Yet, as she had foretold, her child, to which in dying

she had given birth, which breathed not until the mother breathed no more, her child, a daughter, lived. And she grew strangely in stature and intellect, and was the perfect resemblance of her who had departed, and I loved her with a love more fervent than I had believed it possible to feel for any denizen of earth.

But, ere long the heaven of this pure affection became darkened, and gloom, and horror, and grief swept over it in clouds. I said the child grew strangely in stature and intelligence. Strange, indeed, was her rapid increase in

bodily size, but terrible, oh!
terrible were the tumultuous
thoughts which crowded upon
me while watching the
development of her mental
being. Could it be otherwise,
when I daily discovered in the
conceptions of the child the
adult powers and faculties of
the woman? when the lessons
of experience fell from the lips
of infancy? and when the
wisdom or the passions of
maturity I found hourly
gleaming from its full and
speculative eye? When, I say,
all this became evident to my
appalled senses, when I could
no longer hide it from my soul,

nor throw it off from those perceptions which trembled to receive it, is it to be wondered at that suspicions, of a nature fearful and exciting, crept in upon my spirit, or that my thoughts fell back aghast upon the wild tales and thrilling theories of the entombed Morella? I snatched from the scrutiny of the world a being whom destiny compelled me to adore, and in the rigorous seclusion of my home, watched with an agonizing anxiety over all which concerned the beloved.

And as years rolled away, and I gazed day after day upon

her holy, and mild, and
eloquent face, and poured over
her maturing form, day after
day did I discover new points
of resemblance in the child to
her mother, the melancholy
and the dead. And hourly grew
darker these shadows of
similitude, and more full, and
more definite, and more
perplexing, and more
hideously terrible in their
aspect. For that her smile was
like her mother's I could bear;
but then I shuddered at its too
perfect identity, that her eyes
were like Morella's I could
endure; but then they, too,
often looked down into the

depths of my soul with Morella's own intense and bewildering meaning. And in the contour of the high forehead, and in the ringlets of the silken hair, and in the wan fingers which buried themselves therein, and in the sad musical tones of her speech, and above all—oh, above all, in the phrases and expressions of the dead on the lips of the loved and the living, I found food for consuming thought and horror, for a worm that would not die.

Thus passed away two lustra of her life, and as yet my daughter remained nameless upon the earth. "My child," and "my love," were the designations usually prompted by a father's affection, and the rigid seclusion of her days precluded all other intercourse. Morella's name died with her at her death. Of the mother I had never spoken to the daughter, it was impossible to speak. Indeed, during the brief period of her existence, the latter had received no impressions from the outward world, save such as might have been afforded by the narrow limits of her privacy. But at length the ceremony of baptism presented to my mind, in its unnerved and agitated condition, a present deliverance from the terrors of my destiny. And at the baptismal font I hesitated for a name. And many titles of the wise and beautiful, of old and modern times, of my own and foreign lands, came thronging to my lips, with many, many fair titles of the gentle, and the happy, and the good. What prompted me then to disturb the memory of the buried dead? What demon urged me to breathe that sound, which in its very recollection was wont to make ebb the purple blood in torrents from the temples to the heart? What fiend spoke from the recesses of my soul, when amid those dim aisles, and in the silence of the night, I whispered within the ears of the holy man the syllables—Morella? What more than fiend convulsed the features of my child, and overspread them with hues of death, as starting at that scarcely audible sound, she turned her glassy eyes from the earth to heaven, and falling prostrate on the black slabs of our ancestral vault, responded—"I am here!"

Distinct, coldly, calmly distinct, fell those few simple sounds within my ear, and

thence like molten lead rolled
hissingly into my brain.
Years—years may pass away,
but the memory of that epoch
never. Nor was I indeed
ignorant of the flowers and the
vine—but the hemlock and the
cypress overshadowed me
night and day. And I kept no
reckoning of time or place, and
the stars of my fate faded from
heaven, and therefore the earth
grew dark, and its figures
passed by me like flitting
shadows, and among them all I
beheld only—Morella. The
winds of the firmament
breathed but one sound within
my ears, and the ripples upon

the sea murmured evermore— Morella. But she died; and with my own hands I bore her to the tomb; and I laughed with a long and bitter laugh as I found no traces of the first in the channel where I laid the second.—Morella.

Printed in Great Britain
by Amazon

52566258R00020